Simon and the Witch

Collins
RED
STORYBOOK

Also by Margaret Stuart Barry

Simon and the Witch in School
The Millionaire Witch
The Return of the Witch
The Witch on Holiday
The Witch V.I.P.
The Witch and the Holiday Club
The Witch of Monopoly Manor

Margaret Stuart Barry

Simon and the Witch

Illustrated by Linda Birch

CollinsChildren'sBooks
An Imprint of HarperCollinsPublishers

First published in Great Britain by
William Collins Sons & Co. Ltd 1976
First published in Young Lions 1978
This edition published 1995

1 3 5 7 9 8 6 4 2

CollinsChildren'sBooks is a division of
HarperCollins*Publishers* Ltd,
77-85 Fulham Palace Road,
Hammersmith, London W6 8JB

Printed and bound in Great Britain
by HarperCollins Manufacturing Ltd, Glasgow

ISBN 0 00 672064 1

Contents

To Emily with thanks

The Backwards Spell

It was Friday afternoon and Simon was delighted to find his friend the witch waiting for him beside the school gate.

"Hullo," said Simon.

"Hullo," said the witch. "Did you have a good day in school?"

"Very good," said Simon. "I got all my sums right and I got a star for my writing."

"A star?" The witch looked surprised. "How big was it?"

Simon laughed. "Not very big," he said. "It was only a paper one."

"A *paper* one!? That's a fat lot of good! I've got a *real* one at home. It's hanging up in my kitchen – saves electricity you know."

Simon was annoyed at the witch's boasting; he'd worked jolly hard for his star. "That's silly," he said. "A real star wouldn't fit into your kitchen. Real stars are bigger even than this world!"

"How d'you know?" snapped the witch, who hated being contradicted.

"I read it."

"You read it! Huh! Bet you haven't been up there to *see*. Come home with me and I'll show you."

This was the first time the witch had invited Simon to her home and he was terribly excited. He expected her house to be old and dark and covered with cobwebs, with a toadstool for a chimney. But it was a neat semi-detached with a garden full of cabbages and yellow nasturtiums.

"Is this it!?" gasped Simon. He was enormously disappointed.

"What did you expect?" asked the witch," – a dark old house covered with cobwebs with a toadstool for a chimney?"

"Well . . . " began Simon.

"Wipe your feet," said the witch.

It was *exactly* like home.

Inside, there was a television, a gas fire, and a telephone. The only object which was at all witch-like was a rather mean-looking black cat named

George. It looked at him unpleasantly – which was something.

"Now I'll show you my star," said the witch. And she led the way into the kitchen.

There above the cooker was a glistening silver star. It had six sharp points and it twinkled like mad. Simon touched it; it was round and hard and very cold. It was without doubt a real one.

"Told you so, didn't I!" grinned the witch triumphantly. "Of course there *are* lots of stars millions and trillions and billions times bigger than the world. But there are also lots of little ones – if one takes the trouble to search for them."

Simon was beginning to enjoy himself again. He hadn't many friends as interesting as the witch: not any in fact.

"And it must be time for tea," the witch was saying. "What will you have, a little something on toast?"

"Scrambled eggs please," said Simon.

"Scrambled eggs?" asked the witch. "That's not much of a tea for a growing boy. I'm having beetles-all-in-a-turmoil. Very nutritious."

"If you don't mind, I'd prefer scrambled eggs," said Simon. "I'm more used to them."

"Suit yourself," snorted the witch, "but you don't know what you're missing."

When tea was over they sat and watched television for a while and telephoned Simon's mother to say where he was. George clawed the carpet and made enormous holes in it, and the gas fire hissed cosily.

"Have you got a book of spells?" asked Simon at length.

"Of course I have. Why?" asked the witch.

"I'd rather like to have a look."

"What a funny child you are," laughed the witch. And she went to fetch it.

The spell book was just like a recipe book, but much more interesting. Simon couldn't put it down.

"Do you think I could try one?" he asked.

"I suppose you could," agreed the witch. "It's not usual, but I could find you a beginner's spell."

She thumbed through the pages, licking her bony fingers as she turned them over. "Fancy turning anybody into a frog?"

"Is that a *beginner's* spell!?" gasped Simon.

"Oh yes," said the witch. "Everybody, but *everybody* turns somebody into a frog. You must have read about it."

Simon was excited.

The school gardener was not a very close friend of his. He had reported Simon for playing football on the new lawn and Simon had got into trouble. "I'd like to turn the school gardener into a frog," he decided.

"And why not!" exclaimed the witch.

She scribbled out the spell for him on a scrap of paper and said that she would see him another day.

Simon went home and he learnt the spell off by heart. It went –

Cold cabbage, boiled cabbage
School dinner sog,
Eat it with a rubber spoon
And turn into a frog.

"I'm going to turn the school gardener into a frog." Simon told his friends next day.

"Don't be silly," said Sally, who was on Book Four.

"I am, really!" said Simon. "Do you want to watch?"

The children, who had nothing special to do, followed him out through the playground and into the vegetable patch. The school gardener was banking up potatoes.

When he saw Simon he roared, "Gerroff! You little perisher!"

So Simon said,

Cold cabbage, boiled cabbage
School dinner sog,

Eat it with a rubber spoon
And turn into a frog.

At once, the school gardener turned into a slimy green frog and hopped away.

"Well," agreed Sally, "I admit it worked, but you'd better turn him back again or there might be trouble."

"Turn him back again!?" said Simon. "But I don't know how!"

"Then there'll be trouble," said the other children – very pleased – first, because there'd be trouble, and second, because any kind of trouble was better than lessons.

"Please Miss," said Sally "Simon has turned the school gardener into a frog."

"Get on with your work," said the teacher, who was far too clever to believe in magic.

But when a month had passed and nobody had set eyes on the school gardener, the teachers began to believe the story.

Simon was brought before the headmaster whose name was Mr Bodley.

"There's a frog jumping around in the potato patch and we have reason to believe that it's the school gardener," said Mr Bodley, very severely.

"It is," said Simon, who wasn't very good at telling lies.

Mr Bodley frowned heavily. "If he's not back on duty by tomorrow morning, you'll be in serious trouble. You will write one thousand times, *I must not turn school gardeners into frogs."*

Simon trailed home, miserably. He hated writing lines, it made his wrist ache so. After tea he went to see the witch.

"What's up?" asked the witch. "Didn't the spell work?"

"It worked," said Simon. "But there's a lot of bother about it."

"Bother?"

"Yes, the headmaster doesn't like the school gardener being a frog."

"You surprise me," said the witch. "Frogs are very useful in a garden. They catch insects and generally keep things under control. Your headmaster doesn't sound frightfully educated."

"He isn't," confessed Simon, glumly.

"Ah well, crabs to him! I'll find you the backwards spell."

But unfortunately, it wasn't there – just the remains of a torn page.

"Drat!" said the witch. "George must've eaten it, little vandal! Must've been one of those days I forgot his tin of Tabby."

Simon was aghast.

"Don't look so aghast," said the witch. "What's a school gardener here or there? One less won't make much difference."

But Mr Bodley the headmaster didn't see it that way.

"Bring that witch here at once!" he bellowed.

The witch came.

"Take a chair," boomed Mr Bodley.

The witch was very surprised, but she took the chair and ran off with it down the corridor. It was exactly the sort she wanted for her kitchen.

"Come back here," roared Mr Bodley.

The witch came.

"We've a right one here!" she muttered to Simon who was standing in the doorway, "–Says one thing and means another!" She tossed the chair into the corner and sat on Mr Bodley's desk, resting her feet on his knees.

Mr Bodley didn't like that either but he started, " . . . about our school gardener . . . "

"Yes?" said the witch.

The headmaster had a lot of important looking letters on his desk; she made a paper aeroplane out of one of them and it flew beautifully until it got stuck on the picture rail.

" . . . I don't like him being a frog," Mr Bodley went on.

"Who?"

"The school gardener."

"Why ever not?" The witch looked astonished. "What have you got against frogs? I like 'em. Hop hop, croak croak, eat up all the pesky insects."

"That's beside the point," bellowed Mr Bodley.

"And the potato patch," giggled the witch. She pulled out an enormous watch from the folds of her black dress, shook it, and said, "It's eleven o'clock already!"

"What's that got to do with turning my school gardener back into a man?"

"Nothing at all," said the witch. "It just means it's time for coffee. Funny thing that! When I'm thirsty I can never remember a thing. Especially

backwards spells, they're the worst."

Mr Bodley sighed heavily and rang for coffee. The witch drank it greedily.

"And now," said the headmaster, "have you remembered the backwards spell?"

"What backwards spell?" asked the witch. "I

tell you what, the coffee cups in this school are awfully small. I'm not surprised people don't like coming to school. I wouldn't come if you paid me."

Mr Bodley groaned and sent for more coffee.

Soon, the whole of the top of Mr Bodley's desk was covered in coffee cups. His important letters were completely ruined, and his floor was knee deep in paper aeroplanes. And *still* the witch seemed to be having difficulty remembering the backwards spell. Again she pulled out the enormous watch and stared at it.

"Now what's the matter?" groaned the headmaster. He was feeling very weak.

"Nothing's the matter," snorted the witch. "It's twelve o'clock that's all. You do serve dinner here I suppose?"

"Yes," moaned Mr Bodley.

"Well, that's lucky," said the witch. "School dinners are very good for restoring the memory. That's why they were invented."

"I never knew that," said the headmaster, crawling out of his own door on his hands and knees.

The children were delighted to have a witch at dinner. She taught them how to fit fifteen peas on one fork, and how to hide the bits of food they didn't like under their knives. After the rhubarb pie she seemed suddenly to have recovered and led the excited children out to the potato patch. When they had found the frog the witch muttered,

> *"Cold cabbage, boiled cabbage*
> *Flies in the jam,*
> *Drink it from a plastic bucket*
> *And turn into a man."*

At once, the frog turned back into the school gardener and stamped indoors to complain.

"Not a pleasant sight," commented the witch, "but if that's what everybody wants . . . "

For some reason that the children couldn't understand, they were sent home early that afternoon. Simon walked down the road with the witch.

"Did you *really* forget the backwards spell?" he asked.

"Of course I didn't. Witches don't forget things. Now if you've finished asking silly questions I must go home and feed George before he eats my kitchen table."

And off she went.

The Lost Magic Wand

Simon was bored. He'd finished his homework hours ago. All he had to do was to draw a picture of a monster, and as he was very good at drawing monsters it had taken him only five minutes. He began to think about the witch. He thought it was mean of her – the way she kept disappearing for ages – and he was just wondering if he would ever see her again when the phone rang.

"It's for you, dear," called his mother.

Simon ran to the phone and came back again looking pleased.

"Who was it?" his mother asked.

"It was my friend the witch," said Simon. "She wants me to meet her in Mr Valdini's snack bar."

"Oh," said his mother, not believing a word of it. "Well put on your mac, I think it's going to rain."

Oddly enough, the snack bar, which was usually very full, was empty – except for the witch and Mr Valdini.

"Friend of yours, is she?" asked Mr Valdini when Simon came in.

"Yes," said Simon, feeling proud.

"Well she's very bad for business!" Mr Valdini complained. "All my customers have gone. Vamooshed! We're not used to the likes of her."

The witch gave Mr Valdini a malicious glare.

"On the other hand," said Mr Valdini, hastily, "it could just be the weather. It's definitely going to rain."

"Two cokes," said the witch, slamming her plump elbows on the counter.

"That will be twenty pence," said Mr Valdini.

"Twenty pence!" gasped the witch. "I could rent a room in Buckingham Palace for that! I've a good mind to turn your snack bar into an old hen house!"

"Two pence then," gulped Mr Valdini, pouring two cokes and dashing off to see if there were any glasses which needed washing.

"You shouldn't have done that," scolded Simon.

"Done what?" asked the witch.

"Frightened Mr Valdini, he's a friend of mine."

"He's stuck up," snapped the witch. "Forget about him."

When the witch chose, she could be very severe so Simon changed the subject.

"Why did you want to see me?" he asked.

"My life has become extraordinarily dull," began the witch, putting on a very sorry expression.

"Dull?"

"As ditch water," said the witch.

Simon was puzzled.

"But how can your life be dull when you can do magic every day?"

"It wouldn't if I could but I can't – I've lost my magic wand."

"Lost your magic wand!" Simon was aghast.

"Mislaid it completely," wailed the witch. And she began to cry very noisily. Tears bounced from her green eyes until the whole of the front of her dress and most of Mr Valdini's table were sopping wet.

"Please!" begged Simon (he had always found crying a waste of time). "That's not the end of the world."

The witch blew her nose on the tablecloth, sounding very like a trumpet. "Why isn't it?"

she asked.

"I once lost my school satchel and I went to the Police Station and asked for Lost Property."

"Not Lost Satchels?" asked the witch.

"Those as well," said Simon, wanting to laugh. "Anyway, I got my satchel back."

"Property, property," muttered the witch. "That's a nice word. I must try using it sometime."

"We were talking about your wand," reminded Simon.

"So we were," said the witch, and she began to cry again.

"And I said that we should go to the Police Station."

"So you did," said the witch, taking the whole tablecloth as a handkerchief. "Lead the way."

The Police Station was up a hill and round a corner. It was new and smart, and a blue lamp hung over the door.

"Evening," greeted Constable Scuff.

"Yes," agreed Simon and the witch.

"Have you come about last week's murder, tonight's burglary, or tomorrow's possible trouble?" asked Constable Scuff.

"Lost Property," said Simon.

"Oh," said Constable Scuff, disappointed. He was sick and tired of Lost Property – umbrellas, dogs, watches, lost budgies and stray grannies.

" . . . A magic wand," explained Simon.

"Not an umbrella – but a magic wand!" said the Constable, yawning, (He was used to children asking him for silly things).

"A *witch's* magic wand!" said the witch, catching hold of the bored constable by his helmet, so stopping him from falling fast asleep behind his own counter.

Constable Scuff peered over the counter and he could see a pointed hat, a big nose, and two green eyes. A funny feeling like a worm up the back of his vest crept up him.

"I *do* beg your pardon," he said.

At once, murders seemed very unimportant. He was in charge of Missing Magic Wands. "Where did you lose it?" he asked, turning to a brand new page in his notebook.

"If I knew that I wouldn't be asking you!" snapped the witch.

"Quite so," agreed the constable, scribbling all over the empty page as if he'd never heard of the paper shortage and turning to another.

DOES . . . NOT . . . KNOW . . . he wrote.

Meanwhile, the witch was staring hard at Constable Scuff. She greatly admired his navy uniform and his silver buttons. She could just see herself in such a uniform. She already had the

black shoes and stockings! "I want to be a Police-woman," she said.

"Don't be silly," said Constable Scuff, without thinking.

At once, he knew he had made a mistake: the witch caught hold of him by the chain of his whistle and shook him like a box of cornflakes.

"I'll get you a uniform!" gasped the alarmed constable, hurrying off to the storeroom.

Once in uniform, the witch felt that she should be on the other side of the counter, so she climbed over.

"What have we got to do today?" she asked.

Constable Scuff looked up his Crime Book. "There's a fox down at Winterlow Farm stealing chickens," he began.

"Leave that," said the witch. "Foxes have to eat."

"And then there's an unidentified flying object flying around over the airport."

"Probably only my Aunt Matilda," said the witch. "She has no sense of direction."

"Then there are the two thieves who cleaned up half the district."

"Cleaned up?"

"Emptied houses. Stolen stuff," explained the constable.

"Much more interesting!" said the witch. "We'll look for thieves, and perhaps we'll find my wand on the way."

But none of them knew where to start.

"One thing I *do* know," said Constable Scuff.

"Yes?" said Simon and the witch.

"We've got to start looking *somewhere*."

"He's bright, you know, is our Constable Scuff!" scoffed the witch.

They started to look. They looked down dark alleys, along weedy river banks, under oil drums, and in Mr Valdini's snack bar, where they had a cup of coffee. Constable Scuff's transistor began to bleep and he switched it on.

"Tango Delta Romeo," said a voice at the other end.

"Roger," muttered the constable.

This didn't seem to make much sense to the witch so she switched on her transistor and got Top of the Pops.

"You're my Baby Booby Doo," she sang as she rolled out on to the pavement.

It began to pour down, as Simon's mother had said it would and they scrambled into a telephone kiosk and shivered.

"They're not in here anyway," puffed Constable Scuff. And it was such a squash in the kiosk the windows began to steam up.

"We can *all* see that!" leered the witch.

"Let's think," said Simon. So they went back to Mr Valdini's to do it.

"What would you do if you'd stolen a lot of valuable things?"

"Give myself up and hope for leniency," said Constable Scuff.

"Hide under the bed and hold my breath," said the witch.

Simon considered these two answers. He wasn't an awfully quick thinker but he was a hard one.

"They haven't given themselves up," he said at length.

"So they must be hiding under a bed!" exclaimed the witch, gleefully.

"Likely," said Simon, trying very hard to remember what he'd been going to say before he'd started and hoping that no one would interrupt before he had. "But no one could stay under a bed forever. They'd get hungry so what would they do then?"

"Come out and buy fish and chips and then lots of lovely things like a coloured telly and those pot ducks you stick on walls," said the witch.

"Exactly," said Simon. "So we shouldn't be

looking in shabby places at all, but for somewhere smart."

"I *see*!" exclaimed Constable Scuff.

"He *sees*!" sniggered the witch.

They bought an ice lolly each and set off to look for smart looking property.

"*There's* a smart looking house!" exclaimed the witch.

"It's yours," said Simon, "and you knew it was!"

The witch grinned, slyly.

It wasn't easy finding smart looking property. Most of the houses around the town looked as if they could do with a coat of paint and people had taken to patching their curtains to save money. But just past the Public Library loomed a tall block of flats called Ski Hi Court. And there on the fourteenth floor was a bright window filled with orange silk curtains. Constable Scuff whisked out his notebook and wrote, ORANGE . . . SILK . . . CURTAINS. DEAD SUSPICIOUS.

They went up in the lift, and then down again, and up again because the witch loved rides.

"Can we get on with the case?" asked the constable, thinking the witch was very childish but not daring to say so.

The witch pushed her nose through the letter box and arranged her eyes so that she could see

into the flat.

"Oooooooooooooh!" she said.

"What?" said Simon.

"I was right! Posh pot ducks! Flying all over the walls!"

"What else?"

"A coloured telly. There's a football match on!"

"Let me see," said the constable.

"No," said the witch.

"Who's playing?" asked the constable, who was football crazy.

"Spurs against Liverpool. Ooooh!" screeched the witch.

"What? What? What?" groaned the constable.

"That was a foul!"

"*Do* let me have a little look," begged the constable.

"Shan't," snapped the witch. "Go away and solve a murder or something."

"Can't you see anything else?" asked Simon, who thought they were wasting time.

"Hang about," said the witch. "Yes, now I can! There are two men sitting by the fire."

"What do they look like?" the constable wanted to know.

The witch rubbed her nose, which was beginning to ache, and shoved it further through the letter box.

"They're wearing striped jerseys, cloth caps, and black masks over their eyes."

"Typical burglar's gear!" cried Constable Scuff, excitedly. "We've cracked it!"

He kicked down the door, blowing his whistle and waving his truncheon all at the same time, the way he'd been taught.

"Oh dear," groaned the burglars, whose names were Bert and Fred.

"The game's up."

"What about my wand?" said the witch.

"We'll get to that in due course," said the constable importantly, and enjoying himself more hugely than he'd done for a long time.

The flat was full of stolen loot. There was Lady

Fox-Custard's silver rose bowl (presented to her by the Ladies Bowling Club), some expensive plastic chrysanthemums, a tin of luncheon meat, a diamond necklace, and ten bags of sugar.

"Disgusting!" said Constable Scuff.

"Apologies," said Bert, blushing crimson and giving the fire a poke.

"My wand!" screamed the witch. "He's poking the fire with my wand!"

"Wand?" said Bert, muddled, and dropping the "poker" as if it were red hot.

"*Magic* wand!" bellowed the witch, snatching it up.

She changed everything in the room to pure gold, worth about a million billion pounds, and then back again, just to demonstrate.

"Oh cripes!" groaned Bert, "and to think if we'd've known that old stick could've done all that we could've saved ourselves all that lock-picking and stealing around and brain work!"

"Fools!" said Fred.

"Prison!" said Constable Scuff.

"And I should jolly well think so!" said the witch, delighted. And she switched on her police radio and yelled "Roger and out", the way all policewomen talk.

The Witch at the Seaside

It was a warm, blue-sky day, and Simon was sprawled out under the hedge enjoying things. He was wearing his brown sandals, cotton pants, and a waspy-patterned T-shirt.

"Hullo," said the witch, appearing out of nowhere the way she usually did. "Why aren't you in school today – getting more stars?"

"I'm on holiday," beamed Simon.

"On holiday? Get up and let me see!"

Simon rolled over and the witch looked at the spot where he had been lying. All she could see was flattened grass.

"*What* did you say you were on?" she asked.

"Holiday," said Simon.

"Just looks like a lot of flattened grass to me," scowled the witch.

Simon burst out laughing. "Don't you know what a holiday is?"

"Give me a clue," said the witch. "Is it animal, vegetable or mineral?"

"A holiday is something one *has,*" explained Simon.

"Like an alarm clock?"

"Of course not."

"Like a deep freezer?" asked the witch. She liked quiz games.

"No." Simon was becoming confused. "Well you don't just *have* them, sometimes you *go* on them."

"Wheeeeeeeeeeeeeeeee!" chortled the witch. "A motor bike then?"

"Oh dear! Not a motor bike!"

"Bet I'm getting warmer though? A helter-skelter? A helicopter? A dodgem car? An inter-city express? A donkey?"

Now Simon was thoroughly confused. "None of those," he said.

"I give up," said the witch, looking sullen and disheartened.

Simon was about to say that some people *took* a holiday when he changed his mind and said instead that he would take the witch to the seaside

because that is where the best kind of holidays begin.

Happily, it was only a short bus ride to the seaside and the witch was terribly excited. She bounced up and down on the seat all the way. When they arrived, the weather was still very warm and little zig-zags of hot air sizzled up into the sky. They scrambled up a ridge of sand dunes.

"There it is!" cried Simon. "There's the sea."

"Help!" screamed the witch, leaping sky-high with fright and clutching her black dress around her. "A flood!"

"Oh really!" exclaimed Simon, "you go hoofing

off into space, collecting stars and doing other extraordinary things, and then you're dead scared of a bit of water."

"My dear boy," said the witch sternly, "that out there is not 'a bit' as you so innocently put it – it's a whole lot! I can recognize a disaster when I see one, and that's one."

"Listen," said Simon, who was thinking of all the sand pies he wasn't making. "I promise you that the sea will stay where it is. It always does. It won't come rolling all over England and make our houses all awash and drown us."

"You're quite *sure* about that?"

"Quite."

"W . . . . . ell." The witch had been staring all the while at the sea and she had to admit that it looked absolutely super and splendid, and wet as well. "I'll give it a try."

The tide was out, which was good because it left more sand. There was fine dry sand near the promenade and there was flat wet sand further down. Simon had spent all his pocket money on return bus fares so could not afford buckets and spades from the kiosk. He hunted around until he found two empty yoghurt cartons, and except that they did not have pictures of Mickey Mouse on them, they were just as good. He ladled in the sand with his fingers, flattened the top with the palm of his hand, and then turned the carton upside down. Out came a perfect sand pie.

"What's that?" asked the witch.

"It's a perfect sand pie," said Simon.

"Oh." The witch stared at it. "I thought perhaps it was a holiday."

"You make one," suggested Simon.

"It seems like a waste of time," snorted the witch.

"But not if one enjoys it," said Simon, who sometimes said very wise things.

So the witch tried it. And she found it so enjoyable that she simply could not stop. She made sand pies all over the beach, north, south, east and west until she came to a large sand castle which was in the way. She kicked it down.

"That was mine!" exclaimed a little girl who had freckles all over her nose.

"Then you shouldn't have put it there, should you? It was slap bang in the middle of my holiday."

The little girl with freckles on her nose did not cry, she just made her mouth go into a long thin line and gave the witch a hateful look.

Without warning, the witch left her pies and went racing across the beach like a black whirlwind. She returned carrying two ice creams with chocolate flakes stuck in them.

"I didn't know you had any money with you?"

said Simon, his eyes popping.

"I hadn't," said the witch.

"Then how did you get those?"

"Simple," said the witch. "I told the man in the kiosk that I'd turn him into a sea serpent if he didn't hand 'em over. And he said, "d'you want chocolate in 'em or raspberry yukky?"

"That's dishonest!" gasped Simon.

"It's ice cream," grinned the witch, beginning to lick. "Eat yours before the sun gets it."

It was no good trying to do the right thing by returning the ice cream, for it was melting fast, so Simon sat down and ate it.

Just then there came a small sound from behind them. It was a wave smacking the wet sand. The wave toppled over and ran away down the beach, making lacy patterns as it went and rattling the pebbles with it. Then it stopped, took a deep breath, and rushed up the beach again. The witch, who had been watching it in open-mouthed horror, let out a shriek like a force ten gale.

"It's coming after us! You promised it would stay put! I *knew* I knew a disaster when I saw one."

"It's only the tide coming in," cried Simon, running after her and trying to calm her down. "It won't come any further than the prom."

"Oh yes! That's *your* story. I shouldn't have listened to you the first time."

Then all the children began to laugh. They thought the witch was awfully funny.

Laughter! The witch couldn't believe her ears. Merriment in the middle of a disaster – and it was coming from small children, and their parents, aunts and uncles, and a whole assortment of other people. Suddenly the witch grew angry. She wondered why she hadn't thought of it before. She whisked out her magic wand and waved it furiously at the sea. At once, the sea disappeared with a loud sucking noise – like water out of a bath when the soap is blocking the plug hole.

The laughter and the merriment stopped at once and there was a great "oooooooooooh!" from everybody on the beach. The sight which met their eyes was like no other they had ever seen. Thousands of fish lay leaping and gulping on the

empty sea bed. Seaweed of every shape and sort stopped waving and lay still. A ship which had been sailing on the horizon sank down with a heavy glug, keeled over, and all the sailors fell off.

"Titter *now*!" whooped the witch, immensely pleased with her handiwork. "I'm not having *my* house and property all awash."

"But you can't *do* this!" gasped Simon, greatly embarrassed.

"I just did," giggled the witch, starting to make more sand pies.

There was a long silence. And then suddenly there wasn't. Television cameras arrived and

newspaper men. Sam, the manager from the Quick Frozen Fish Factory, drove up and started to collect the flapping fish in huge binfuls. Then Sergeant Friskum from the local police station appeared.

"'Ullo 'ullo 'ullo," said Sergeant Friskum, whipping out his notebook in readiness. "And what 'ave we 'ere?"

"One English Channel. Missing," said an onlooker.

"Missing you say?" said the sergeant, writing lots of notes. "And does anybody 'ere present know who dunnit?"

"*She* did," said the little girl with freckles all

over her nose.

"I saw her. She took out this stick thing and she waved it at the sea and it went."

"I see," said the sergeant, going into a frenzy of note writing.

"I shall have to apprehend her."

Everybody waited breathlessly, wondering what the witch would do when she was apprehended. But all she did was to make more sand pies.

The sergeant was non-plussed, which meant he didn't know what to do next. "We just can't have this sort of thing," said Sergeant Friskum, lamely.

"Ring Scotland Yard," said the little girl with freckles all over her nose.

"I will, I will," said the sergeant, glad of an excuse to drive away.

The television cameramen wanted to take pictures of the witch. The witch liked that a lot. She took off her hat, brushed her hair, and then sat, posing, in the middle of her sand pies. Simon noticed this with interest. It gave him an idea.

"I daresay," he started casually, "that if you were to put the sea back again, the television men could take pictures of you doing it, then we could dash home and watch it on the news."

"In colour?" asked the witch, not wanting to

look too pleased too soon.

"Definitely," said one of the cameramen

"And I want to go home in a taxi, not on the bus."

"That can be arranged," said the cameraman.

So the witch waved the sea back, climbed into the taxi and went home. Simon put the kettle on and the witch toasted some crumpets, then they both sat down to watch the news.

The missing sea, and its return, was the first item to be shown.

"There's ME! ! !" squealed the witch. "Don't I look great?"

"Yes," said Simon.

"Let's have another holiday tomorrow."

"Er . . . . . . my mother's taking me to buy new shoes tomorrow," said Simon. "Another time perhaps."

The Witch has Measles

Days passed, and then weeks, and Simon didn't see the witch at all. Then it occurred to him that perhaps there might be something wrong and he had better go and see.

As soon as he approached her garden gate he knew that he had been right: there were forty-nine milk bottles on the witch's doorstep and forty-nine copies of the Echo Evening News.

"I wonder which is the more stupid – the milkman or the paper boy?" said Simon aloud.

He rang the bell and nobody told him to come in. He went round to the back door and peered through the kitchen window. All he could see was a pile of dirty dishes in the sink and a great

deal of dust everywhere.

"This looks serious," said Simon. And he opened the door and went in. The witch was not watching television, and not reading her spell book, and not doing anything. She wasn't there.

"Oh dear," said Simon. "I do hope she hasn't gone. Perhaps she's left the country altogether!"

He went upstairs to see if there were any clues in the bedroom and he found the witch in bed.

"You shouldn't have rushed over here so quickly," complained the witch. She was completely covered in spots.

"You've got spots all over you!" exclaimed Simon.

"My goodness, you're sharp!" snapped the witch. "Of course I have: I've got Double German Measles."

Simon laughed. "One can't have *double* German Measles!" he said.

"Don't tell me what I can't have when I've got them!" said the witch, peevishly.

Just then, George walked in, carrying his tail erect like a black flag. He too was covered in spots.

"He's got it as well!" cried Simon.

George gave Simon a withering look and started to munch hungrily at the bedspread.

"Poor beast, he's starving," said the witch. "You didn't happen to notice if the milkman had left any milk?"

Simon didn't want to upset the witch by telling her that she had forty-nine bottles of it, so he went downstairs, made a milky coffee for the witch, a bowl of porridge for George, and wrote a note for the milkman saying,

NO MILK UNTIL XMAS, PLEASE.

"Shall I change your sheets?" he asked, wanting very much to be helpful.

"Don't be foolhardy," said the witch. "They were changed only six weeks ago. Do you imagine I'm made of laundry money?"

Simon fell silent. He must do something for his friend the witch. She needed some sort of medical attention he felt. Yet . . .

"What about your wand?" he asked. "Couldn't you use it to – er, tidy up the house a bit and get yourself better?"

The witch raised her eyes to the ceiling in exasperation and her eyeballs rattled around her head like balls in a fruit machine. "You haven't noticed then?" she said.

"Noticed what?" asked Simon.

The witch rolled her eyes even more until they showed two pears and a plum – "My wand has Double German Measles too!" she spat.

Simon looked around until he spotted the witch's wand on a bed-side table. It was encrusted with red measle spots.

"It's encrusted with red measle spots," said the witch.

"I think you should have a doctor," said Simon. "Which doctor do you have?"

"Witch doctor? There's not one I know of this side of Zanzibar."

"There's Doctor Macrae. He lives just down the road. I had him when I had measles."

"That would be *single* measles I suppose?" said the witch.

"Yes," agreed Simon.

"Well phone him," said the witch. "I don't want to die so young."

Doctor Macrae arrived with his black bag. He listened to the witch's chest and examined George's nose and whiskers. "Definitely Double German Measles," he said. "The worst case I've seen."

"Told you, didn't I!" said the witch, looking pleased.

"I'm afraid we'll have to move you to hospital," said Doctor Macrae.

"In an ambulance?"

"Certainly," said the doctor.

"Will they flash the blue light and go – 'nair nur nair nur'?"

"I'm sure I don't know," said Doctor Macrae, leaving hastily.

The ambulance arrived and it flashed its blue light and went nair nur nair nur, at break-neck speed all the way to the Upper Weston General Hospital.

"Into bed you pop. And take your hat off," said a little nurse in a starched pinny.

The witch leaped into the bed but she would not take off her hat.

"Nobody else is wearing a hat," whispered Simon.

"More fool they!" snorted the witch. "It would be imprudent to remove my hat when I am so ill."

Simon groaned. Everyone was staring at his friend.

The nurse came back and stuck a thermometer under the witch's tongue.

She crunched it up and scowled. "I hope all the meals aren't going to be as nasty as that," she grumbled.

Mrs Bundy in the next bed started to titter and Simon said that he had better be going home and would see her later.

The witch began to unpack. She put her toothbrush in a mug, her slippers under a chair, her wand inside her locker, and George on the end of her bed

"Lor sakes!" gasped Mrs Bundy in the next bed. "They won't let you keep that animal in here!"

And all the nurses and the doctors, and even Matron said the same thing. But George arched his back and spat. And he looked so dreadful like that – with all his measle spots as well, that everyone hurried away and didn't mention the subject again.

A woman from the kitchen came in. She was carrying a note book and pencil and she was going from bed to bed. When she came to the witch she said, "Hullo dearie. What would you like for lunch today? We've got boiled beef, roast lamb, and watercress salad."

"I fancy earwig pie," said the witch.

"Oh you are a caution!" giggled the kitchen lady. "I think it's just lovely when the patients make jokes. Now we've got boiled beef and . . . "

"Are you *deaf* or something!?" screeched the witch. "I said I fancied earwig pie. And I want ladybird sauce on it too. Not too much pepper."

Then the kitchen lady got very upset and flew out of the ward, crying.

Matron arrived. And she fluttered her frilly hat and looked red and fierce. "You are being a great bother!" she boomed at the witch. "One more word out of you and I'll send you home – Double German Measles or no German Measles."

The witch pulled her hat down over her eyes and pretended to be asleep.

That evening, Simon came back.

"Are you all right?" he asked.

"Yes. It's like Butlin's Holiday Camp in here," said the witch. "The food is wonderful and the view is terrific. I must send postcards to all my friends."

"I'm so glad," said Simon. And he went home again.

Next day was little better. The witch was given a new thermometer for breakfast, and another for elevenses. She wondered if so much glass was healthy. The Matron boomed so much she made herself ill and had to go and lie down.

"It's not much fun in here is it?" said the witch. "Just look at everybody: all miserably mumbully."

"There not well," explained Mrs Bundy.

"They're bored," said the witch.

Just then, two porters pushed a trolley down the ward and took one of the ladies away on it.

"Did you see that!" cried the witch. They give rides in here – on go-carts!"

"It was a trolley," laughed Mrs Bundy. "And it was only taking Mrs Jones down to have a new bandage on her toe."

"Are there any more of those things around?"

The witch was pink with excitement.

"Yes. There are six of them in the corridor outside."

The witch counted on her fingers. "Six! We could have races!"

"Go to sleep," said Mrs Bundy.

"I will not!" squealed the witch. "Get out of bed and help me bring them in here."

Mrs Bundy was an obliging sort of woman, as well as being just a teeny bit scared of the witch, so she climbed out of bed and helped to bring in the trolleys.

"But who's going to push?" she asked.

"Nobody," said the witch. "Watch me."

She tucked up her nightie, took a long run, and leaped on to the trolley tummy downwards. The trolley sailed smoothly down the ward until the wall at the other end stopped it.

Several of the sick ladies sat up and looked wistfully at the witch. She seemed to be having such great fun.

"But we'll get into awful trouble!" said Mrs Toogood.

"Oh to heck with that!" said Granny who was a hundred and one and felt she hadn't much time left in which to get into trouble. She tottered down the ward to bag herself a trolley.

Then all the other ladies started putting on

their slippers and dressing gowns and fighting for trolleys.

"Wheeeeee!" giggled Granny, as she raced down the ward knocking flowers, bananas, and bottles of orange juice everywhere.

Everybody won a race at least once. The witch won five times, and Granny won six.

"Stop! ! ! " called the witch.

"What?" asked Granny, lying on the floor, helpless with laughter.

"If we tie sheets on the trolleys, they'll be like sailing boats and we can go lots faster," said the witch.

"Great idea," agreed everyone.

And they started pulling sheets off the beds and fixing them to the trolleys with crutches and anything else they could find. After that, the trolleys went so fast that no one had time to see who was winning.

"Oh my goodness!" gasped Granny. "It's a hundred years since I had such fun!"

"Stop! ! ! ! "

"Yes yes! What now?" asked Granny, so delighted she could hardly breathe.

But it was not the witch speaking this time. It was Matron. Her frilly hat had un-frilled itself and lay on the top of her head like a dead seagull.

"I have never, never, NEVER seen such disgraceful behaviour!" she was saying.

The ladies lay very still on their trolleys and tried to look as if they were just about to go down and have their toes bandaged, or something.

"I have never . . . . . " went on Matron.

"Oh do stop saying 'never' will you," cried Granny. "You and your rotten pills wot never worked. I'm going home. I feel so much better!"

"Eureka!" yelled the witch.

"What is it?" cried everyone.

"My spots have gone!"

She looked at her cat and her wand. They were spotless too.

"Shall I change Matron into a super trolley?" she grinned.

"No," said the ladies. "She's quite nice really when one gets to know her."

"All right then," said the witch, "I won't this time." And she went home.

At visiting time, Simon arrived. When he saw the empty bed he was horrified.

"She's gone home," explained Mrs Bundy.

"Does that mean she's better?" he asked.

"Better than anyone we've ever had before," agreed all the ladies.

"Oh good," said Simon. "I was terribly worried about her."

Halloween

Simon and the witch were sitting in front of the witch's fire, roasting chestnuts on a shovel.

"Do you know what day it is tomorrow?" said Simon.

"It's Saturday," said the witch.

"Yes, but as well as Saturday."

"What do you mean – 'as *well* as Saturday'? Either tomorrow's Saturday or it isn't, it can't be 'as well as'."

Simon looked confused. "What I meant was . . ." he began.

"Then you should have said so in the first place," scolded the witch.

"I meant," Simon went on, "that tomorrow is

Halloween."

"Hallo who?" asked the witch.

"Ween," said Simon.

"So what happens then?"

"Oh lots of things," said Simon. "We have parties and play Duck Apple. Then we cut out the insides of turnips, put candles in them, and carry them through the streets."

"What for?" asked the witch.

Simon could see that his friend the witch was in one of her awkward moods where she was going to ask lists of questions.

"Something to do with power cuts?" the witch went on.

"Of course not," said Simon. "It's just fun. And nice and scarey. And another thing, witches come out of hiding and fly around the sky."

"Which witches?"

"It's just a game," laughed Simon. "They aren't *real.*"

"Not real eh?" said the witch, her eyes suddenly turning very green and beginning to roll as if some very exciting thought was dashing around inside her head.

"All just a game," Simon laughed again. And he went home because he had a lot to do before the party on Saturday.

The Halloween party was to be held in the Town Hall and the Mayor was to give out prizes for the best costumes. Sally who was on Book Four was cutting out black paper and rolling it up into a pointed hat, and most of the other girls were doing the same, although not as neatly as Sally of course.

Simon's mother had an old fur coat she didn't want, and Simon decided that it would make a super cat costume. He spread it on the floor, rolled up in it, stitched it down the middle, wriggled out of it, and hung the costume carefully on the end of his bed.

Next day, Simon's mother made five dozen jam

tarts and took them down to the Town Hall. There were already lots of other mothers there and they had all been making things too. The Mayor was wearing his gold chain and it was so heavy it weighed his head forwards which made it appear that he was getting ready to eat all the jam tarts and the sausage rolls and the jellies before the others had a chance.

Sally arrived in her black pointed hat and she was furious to find that most of the other girls were wearing exactly the same thing. Then Simon came prowling through the doorway, miaowing loudly, and was just as cross to see that his costume too had been copied.

"Copy cat!" he hissed at Jimmy Watson who was pussy-footing around in an old fur of *his* mother's.

All this time, the witch was making her own preparations. She had changed her socks and brushed her dress. Now she was trying to drag George away from the television. George was annoyed because he was trying to watch Tom and Jerry. He didn't want to go to a party. He thought parties were silly and noisy and only for people with very small brains. So the witch turned the television set into a jar of marmalade, tucked George under her arm, and set off down the road.

It was a bright windy night. The moon raced

around the clouds. Or rather, the clouds raced around *it*, and the bare trees thrashed around like gigantic broomsticks. Soon, they could see the lights of the Town Hall.

"We'll wait in this one," said the witch, flying up into a large elm tree. George sat on a branch, sulking. He thought the whole thing was very stupid.

They sat in the elm tree for about an hour and a half.

"D'you know what," said the witch at length (George sniffed and moved further along the

branch). "I think this Halloween story is just one massive leg pull."

George was about to suggest they went home and watched television when a hundred witches, accompanied by their cats, arrived from behind a cloud and settled on the elm tree. I don't know whether you have ever heard rooks at nesting time, but that is how the witches sounded – caw caw, cackle cackle. If the band in the Town Hall had not been playing very loudly, everybody would have come dashing out to see what was the matter.

"Then *you* must be Winnie from Wapping!" the witch was exclaiming, excitedly.

"The very same!" said the other witch. "Which makes Gertie over there your second cousin, and Hatty the Howl your great-great-grandmother."

"Fancy that!" cried the witch. "So we are really all related to one another!"

"Indisputably," said Winnie.

"What a turn up for the books! You must all come round for a meal one day."

"Delighted to," said all hundred witches together. And the elm tree groaned under the weight.

Then the witch remembered the Halloween party. "There's a party we must go to in the Town Hall, but I'm afraid none of the children believes in us."

"We have the same trouble every year," said Gertie. "We were seriously thinking of packing the whole job in. I mean we have better things to do than fly around the chimney pots, catching pneumonia, for the amusement of children who don't believe in us anyway!"

"On the other hand," said the witch, craftily, "there are prizes at this party. And refreshments too."

At this, the witches fell out of the tree in a big heap and started running and flying towards the Town Hall.

"Good heavens!" said Sally when she saw them, "fancy all those old ladies entering the competition. That's not fair!"

"I don't recognize a single one of them," complained the Mayor. "There must be a coach trip in."

"It's not fair!" grumbled all the children.

"Now then," scolded Simon's mother, "we must be hospitable. Pass round the jam tarts."

She'd hardly said it when the tarts were gone.

"Oh!" said everybody, shocked.

"Tasty, those," said the witches, licking their fingers.

The Mayor decided that he had better get on with the judging: he had an uncomfortable feeling that things weren't going too well.

The band began to play again and everyone marched round and round whilst the Mayor judged and judged and consulted the Ladies on the Committee. It wasn't a very large hall in which to march, and with the hundred extra cats who kept wandering willy nilly out of order, people kept stumbling. Sarah Grimshaw stood on her own dress, ripped it, and had to be taken away to the cloakroom in tears.

"That's one less!" giggled Gertie as she stamped along. She could not remember *when* she had enjoyed a party more.

"It's so difficult." The Mayor mopped his brow.

"I must say those old ladies look very realistic in their costumes."

"And the cats are so good," said Mrs Smythe.

"Well *I* think a child should win it," objected Lady Fox-Custard. "After all, we didn't invite all these strangers."

"Who do you think they are then?" asked the Mayor, nervously.

"Some Ladies Sewing Circle – from Upper Scunton I shouldn't wonder," said Lady Fox-Custard.

The Mayor made his mind up very quickly and gave the first "cat" prize to Jimmy Watson and the first "witch" prize to Sally.

He was immediately sorry.

"*Cheat*!" screeched Hatty the Howl. "*She's* not a witch! If *you're* a fair judge, I'm a bottle of black ink!"

The Mayor's gold chain quivered. "Well it's too late now," he said, "I've given the prizes."

"To a silly girl in a paper hat all stuck together with sellotape!" cried Hatty. We are all *professional* witches."

"Now then, ladies," said the Mayor, wishing he were filling his hot water bottle and getting ready for bed, "a joke's a joke and we think your costumes are very good indeed, but all good things come to an end and you'll miss your coach if you don't hurry."

At this the witches huddled together in the middle of the floor, like a great pile of black tents, and they muttered and muttered and discussed this whole turn of events. And all anybody could see was the occasional green eye glinting out from the pile and the odd sharp nose.

"It's obvious," Winnie from Wapping was whispering, "that we shall have to prove ourselves to these unbelieving people."

"How?" hissed Hatty.

"Have they ever seen sausage rolls running round on legs?" asked Winnie.

"I doubt it," said the others.

"Have they seen jellies doing the Rock and Roll?"

"I shouldn't think so."

"Could *they* raise themselves up from the floor and fly around the light bulbs?"

"Never, I'm sure," agreed the others.

"Well then," said Winnie, "it's against my principles to give childish demonstrations, but I think just for once we'll have to."

"We'll have to," said all the witches.

And so they did.

Lady Fox-Custard screamed.

"Ladies Sewing Circle indeed!" said the Mayor, dodging a troupe of wild sausage rolls which ran between his legs.

"Well how was I to know they were real witches? I don't . . . didn't believe in them," wailed Lady Fox-Custard.

"Ooops!" gasped Mrs Smythe, as a yellow jelly ran up her back and disappeared under her hat.

Witches hung from every light fitting, they slid down the pipes, flew in and out of the windows, had broomstick races, and changed all the tables into trampolines.

Suddenly the children began to laugh.

The witches liked that. All witches like showing off. They began to show off more than ever.

"Who's for lemonade?" hooted Hatty. And she changed all the tap water into lemonade.

"This is absolutely great!" cried Simon.

"There'll be complaints from the Water Board," warned the Mayor.

But nobody was listening to him.

Anything the children wanted, the witches produced. Winnie from Wapping started frying fish and chips in her hat. And Hatty the Howl gave free broomstick rides.

"I used to be frightened of witches," laughed Sarah Grimshaw, as she clung on to the back of Hatty the Howl's dress.

"Silly little girl," said Hatty.

But at last it was time to go home, because "going home" is the most perfect of all inventions.

Everyone said "Goodbye" and "It's been lovely meeting you," and that sort of thing.

Simon and the witch walked slowly down the road. The moon had moved a lot and was hanging low behind a church spire.

"I'm glad you met all your relations," Simon was saying.

"Yes," said the witch. "It's nice having a bit of family." She chuckled. "We didn't half show 'em tonight didn't we!?"

"You did. But . . . . . ."

"But what?" said the witch.

"I expect by tomorrow the children will have forgotten all about you."

The witch scowled, and then she laughed. "Better that way perhaps," she said.

And she vanished.

The Witch's Visitor

Simon was very excited because it was nearly Christmas and because Aunty Maggy and Uncle Bill were coming to stay. As if this were not exciting enough, thick snow had fallen during the night and Simon was shovelling a path down to the gate.

The witch appeared with her usual suddenness.

"We're having visitors," explained Simon, shovelling happily.

"What for?" asked the witch, throwing lumps of snow where Simon had just cleared.

"Because it's Christmas, of course," said Simon. "Everyone has visitors at Christmas. Aren't *you* having a visitor?"

"Of course I am," lied the witch, who wasn't at all.

"I'm glad," said Simon. "Have you got your house ready?"

"Ready for what!?" snapped the witch.

"For Christmas of course. You know – decorations, and balloons, and a tree."

"A *tree*! – In the *house*!? That's daft!" said the witch.

"Come on," said Simon, "I'll help you. You can't have a visitor without decorations up."

He collected what was left over from his own tree and went home with the witch.

In her garden was a small oak tree. She pulled it up by the roots and took it indoors. Simon didn't like to say that it didn't look very Christmassy, so he hung lots of tinsel on it and hid it under a pile of red and yellow balloons.

"It looks very silly," snarled the witch, but all the same, she couldn't stop staring at it.

"Now," said Simon, busily, "have you ordered the turkey?"

"Ordered it to do *what*?" The witch was puzzled: she didn't even *own* a turkey. What would be the use of keeping a bird around the place when she had a cat? – George would just have eaten it.

"Never mind," laughed Simon. "Let's go back

to my garden and build a snowman." He was in a very Christmassy mood.

The witch enjoyed the making of the snowman very much. Snow was lovely stuff; crunchy and cold and lots of it. Simon brought out his father's old hat, scarf, and a bubble pipe. For eyes, nose, mouth, and buttons, he used little pieces of coal.

The snowman looked extremely important.

"Better be going in now," Simon said. "By the way," he called as he reached the kitchen door, "Who did you say was coming to visit you?"

"Uncle Fred," said the witch. And she went home.

But when she arrived at her own house, she began to worry. She didn't even *have* an uncle – let alone an uncle called Fred. "Christmas!" she spat. "What a silly invention! What a fuss and bother about nothing. Pah!" Yet, her oak tree looked very fancy and everybody around the town seemed to be having enormous fun.

Scowling horribly, the witch crept back to Simon's house to see what exactly he was up to. She lay on her tummy in the snow and pushed her long nose through the hedge, watching. Aunty Maggy and Uncle Bill were just getting out of a taxi and they had armfuls of presents and boxes of crackers and Christmas puddings.

"Huh! Christmas!" spat the witch again, getting crosser and crosser because there was no such person as Uncle Fred which meant he wouldn't be coming to stay. Rolling around in the snow in

a very bad temper, the witch caught sight of Simon's snowman. She lay with her legs in the air and looked at him for a very long time. He was certainly a very handsome gentleman. He wore his hat at a jaunty angle and without a doubt he knew how to look important.

"My Uncle Fred!" exclaimed the witch.

She snatched out her magic wand and brought the snowman to life.

"Happy Christmas," greeted Uncle Fred, taking the pipe out of his mouth and bowing with great dignity.

"No time for good manners," hissed the witch, glancing craftily in the direction of the house. "We've a bus to catch. Hurry!"

The queue at the bus stop was very long so the witch decided to stand at the front of it.

"Hey!" shouted everybody.

The witch told them that there was a bus strike and that if they wanted to get home in time for Christmas day they'd better start walking.

Mumbling and muttering, the queue shuffled off which meant that when the bus arrived the witch and Uncle Fred were the only people there.

"Room for two inside but no snowmen," bellowed the conductor.

"Is that in the book of rules?" shrieked the witch.

The conductor took out his book of rules and although he shoved back his hat and scratched his head a lot, he just could *not* find the rule which said "No snowmen allowed". He was quite sure he'd seen it because he could remember showing it to one of his mates and laughing and saying, "As if a perishing snowman would want to get on a bus! Ha ha."

"Well?" said the witch.

"Can't find it," said the conductor.

"Thought not," said the witch, looking especially sly and ting-a-linging the bell.

Everybody on the bus was very glad when the witch and her Uncle Fred at last got off. They had never had such a shivery journey.

Meanwhile, George had built up a big fire. He had also eaten half the Christmas tree but this was only because once again the witch had forgotten to leave out his cat food.

"Well, not to worry!" said the witch. "This is Uncle Fred."

George was expected to say, "Happy Christmas Uncle Fred and welcome," but being a witch's cat he said neither and went on munching tinsel from the Christmas tree.

It was Christmas Eve and the snowman was glad to sit by a warm fire. George, smiling his best cat smile, heaped more coal on the fire and shoved

Uncle Fred's chair nearer to the heat.

"Much obliged," said Uncle Fred, and he sat up late – waiting for Father Christmas to come down the chimney and warming his freezing toes by the flames. The longer Uncle Fred waited, the thinner he grew. His hat fell around his eyes, his pipe fell on to the floor, and his scarf drooped around his middle. He was only *just* in time to see Father Christmas's sooty feet landing in the hearth.

"Happy Christmas!" said Father Christmas, putting a box of chocolate spiders and a packet of fish fingers on the rug.

"And a happy Christmas to you too!" said Uncle Fred, melting into a small warm puddle

Christmas morning came with bells and more snow and Simon arrived with presents.

"Where's your Uncle Fred?" he asked.

The witch looked at the floor of the hearth. There was a hat, a scarf, a bubble pipe, and a small heap of coal.

"He had to leave suddenly," she explained.

"Oh," said Simon, disappointed, "well never mind – a very happy Christmas!"